DISNEP
GRAVITY FALLS

PINING AWAY

Adapted by Tracey West

Based on the series created by Alex Hirsch

Part One is based on the episode "Double Dipper,"
written by Michael Rianda, Tim McKeon, Alex Hirsch.

Part Two is based on the episode "The Hand That
Rocks the Mabel," written by Zach Paez, Alex Hirsch.

DISNEP
XD

DISNEP PRESS
New York • Los Angeles

Printed in the United States of America
First Edition
1 3 5 7 9 10 8 6 4 2
V475-2873-0-14157

Library of Congress Control Number: 2014936537
ISBN 978-1-4847-1139-2

For more Disney Press fun, visit www.disneybooks.com
Visit DisneyChannel.com

SUSTAINABLE
FORESTRY
INITIATIVE

Certified Chain of Custody
Promoting Sustainable Forestry

www.sfiprogram.org
SFI-01054

The SFI label applies to the text stock

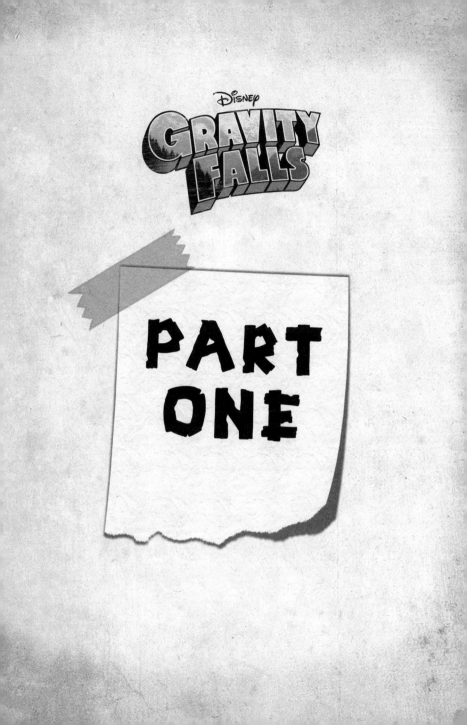

CHAPTER ONE

"**OH NO, MABEL,** I don't feel so good,"
Dipper said, groaning. He made a retching sound
and . . . shot a spray of pink party string at his
twin sister's face!

"Ugh!" Mabel cried. Then she grabbed her stomach. "Grunkle Stan! What did you feed us?"

She picked up a can of purple party string and aimed it at her brother, spraying him with it. Then they both started cracking up.

Their friend Wendy walked up to them. "Guys! Guys! Something terrible happened."

Worried, Dipper and Mabel stopped laughing for a second. Then Wendy pretended to barf green party string all over them.

"Comedy gold!" Mabel exclaimed, tossing confetti into the air. It landed on Stan's head as he walked by.

Stan wasn't amused.

"All right, all right! Party supplies are now off-limits," he said, snatching the party string and confetti from them.

Dipper and Mabel couldn't help being in a good mood. They were looking forward to the party their great-uncle Stan would be holding at his Mystery Shack. At the start of summer, Dipper and Mabel had come to Oregon to stay with their great-uncle at his shack. Nestled deep in the woods, the dusty shack was filled with strange and unusual objects, including dinosaur skulls, ancient carvings, and jars of what looked like eyeballs in liquid. The unusual items brought in the tourists, and Stan hoped they dropped all their money in the souvenir shop on the way out.

Helping out at the shack was interesting, but so far they hadn't met too many new friends except for Wendy and Soos, who worked at the shack, and Old Man McGuckett—who was certifiably insane.

So when Grunkle Stan announced that he was having a party and inviting all of the kids in Gravity Falls, Dipper and Mabel were excited. They spent the afternoon helping spruce up the place for the party. Wendy had blown up some balloons, and Soos hung streamers across the room.

"Mr. Pines, whose birthday is it, again?" Soos asked Stan.

"Nobody's," Stan replied. "I thought this party might be a good way to get kids to spend money at the shack."

He proudly unrolled an old Pin the Tail on the Donkey poster.

"Nice!" Soos said.

"The young people in this town want fun? I'll smother 'em with fun!" said Stan.

Soos might have been impressed, but Dipper knew that his Grunkle Stan was a little, well, out of touch.

"Maybe comments like that are why kids
don't come to the Mystery Shack," Dipper said,
pouring a cup of Diet Pitt Cola for Mabel.

"Hey, hey!" Stan said, grabbing the soda bottle
from him. "How about you make yourself useful
and copy these fliers?"

He handed Dipper a clipboard with fliers on it
that read PARTY AT THE MYSTERY SHACK. KIDS AND
TEENAGERS WELCOME. FREE?

"Oh boy!" said Mabel. "A trip to the copier store!"

Soos popped up behind her. "Calendars, mugs, T-shirts, and more! They got it all at the copier store!" he said in a singsong voice. "That's not their slogan. I just really feel that way about the copier store."

"Save the trouble," Stan said. "You know that old copier in my office? I finally fixed the old girl up. Good as new!"

So they headed off to the shack's dank and dusty storage room. They pulled the cover off the copy machine and moths fluttered out.

Mabel gasped. "Butterflies!"

The copier looked like a hunk of junk. It was covered in dust, dented all over, and held together with duct tape.

"Does it even work?" Dipper asked. He lifted the lid and leaned on the glass so that he could press a button on the control panel.

The copier turned on, and the glass lit up with

a green glow. The machine whirred and scanned Dipper's arm.

Poof! The machine sparked, and clouds of black smoke poured out. When the smoke cleared, a piece of paper slid out onto the tray, showing a clear image of Dipper's arm.

"Success!" Mabel said, picking up the paper.

Suddenly, the paper moved in Mabel's hand. Startled, she dropped it. It fell to the floor, and the copy of Dipper's arm began to change. First, color crept into the black-and-white image. Then the picture transformed into a real-life 3-D arm and started to rise from the paper!

"Aaaaaah!" Dipper and Mabel screamed.

The arm lifted itself straight up in the air, then slammed down onto the floor, dragging itself toward a terrified Dipper and Mabel. The arm crawled closer . . . and closer . . . and closer. . . .

"Stay back!" Dipper yelled. Then he grabbed Mabel's soda and tossed it onto the arm.

The arm began to bubble and sizzle. Then it completely disintegrated. Dipper turned to his sister.

"Oh my gosh, Mabel. I think this copier can copy human beings!"

"Do you realize what this means?" Mabel asked. "Blaaaaaaah!"

Then she
zapped him
in the face
with purple
party string.

CHAPTER TWO

DIPPER AND MABEL didn't bother to tell Grunkle Stan about the creepy copier. They had encountered lots of strange things there in the woods of the Pacific Northwest, but Stan said he didn't believe any of the stories. Sure, he ran a Mystery Shack filled with mystical items, but those were just for gullible tourists.

So Dipper and Mabel finished copying the fliers and took them back to Stan in the party room. Everything looked party-ready, from the strings of lights and balloons to the purple metallic star ornaments. The dance floor was polished to perfection and ready for dancing. Grunkle Stan gathered his party team around him: Dipper, Mabel, Soos, and Wendy.

"Okay, party people—and Dipper," he said, and Dipper frowned. "Let's talk business. Soos, because you'll work for free, and you begged, I'm letting you be DJ."

"You won't regret it, Mr. Pines," Soos said. "I got this book to teach me how to DJ r-r-r-ight."

Soos held up the book: HOW TO DJ R-R-R-R-IGHT BY DJ SCRATCH TRAX.

"Not encouraging," Stan said. "Wendy, you and Mabel are working the ticket stand."

"What?" Mabel cried. "But, Grunkle Stan, this party is my chance to make new friends!"

"I can work with Wendy," Dipper said quickly.

His heart beat a little faster as he said it. He'd had a crush on Wendy ever since he first saw her. He knew it was probably hopeless; she was fifteen, and he wasn't even technically a teenager yet. And she was taller than him. And always seemed to have a boyfriend. But still ... he kept on pining away.

"You do realize if you do, you gotta commit to staying at the ticket stand with Wendy," Stan said firmly. "No getting out of it. Just the two of you. Alone. All night."

Dipper glanced over at Wendy. She was spray-painting a funny face on Soos's belly. He wiggled it to make the face move, and Wendy and Mabel cracked up.

Dipper sighed. Wendy was the girl of his dreams!

"I promise," he told Stan.

Dipper didn't have much time. He ran up to the room he and Mabel shared in the attic of the Mystery Shack. First he needed a plan. Then he needed to make himself look good for Wendy. He was gargling with mouthwash when Mabel walked up and startled him. "Ah! What?" he asked.

Mabel grinned and started to talk in a goofy guy voice. "Uh, I can work the counter with you, Wendy. Let's kiss!" She made kissing noises.

"Yeah, yeah, laugh all you want." Dipper straightened his bow tie in the mirror. "But I have devised a plan to make sure my night with Wendy goes perfect."

"Plan? You're not making one of those over-complicated listy things, are you?" Mabel asked.

"It's not overcomplicated," Dipper insisted. He took the list from his pocket and unfolded it . . . and unfolded it . . . and unfolded it. It was so long that it touched the floor. "'Step six: getting to know each other with playful banter.' Banter is like talking, but smarter."

"That sounds like a dumb idea for poop heads," said Mabel.

"See, this isn't banter," said Dipper, gesturing from himself to Mabel. "This is what I want to avoid with Wendy. The final step is to ask her to dance." Then Dipper grinned as he imagined a perfect night with Wendy:

Wendy and Dipper were on the dance floor, dancing to a slow song.

"Oh, Dipper!" Wendy exclaimed as he dipped her. "I'm so happy you decided to work the ticket

stand with me. You're so organized! Show me that checklist again."

Dipper pulled his long checklist from his pocket.

Wendy swooned as Dipper's fantasy dissolved.

"If I follow steps one through eleven," he said, "nothing can get in my way!"

"Dipper, *you're* the one getting in your way," Mabel told him. "Why can't you just walk up and talk to her like a normal person?"

"Step nine, Sister!" Dipper said triumphantly, pointing to the list: Step 9: TALK LIKE A NORMAL PERSON.

Mabel shook her head. Her brother was hopeless!

The twins went downstairs. Dipper headed outside to the ticket booth, where lots of kids were lined up to enter the dance. Inside, Soos was playing tunes while a glittery disco ball spun from the ceiling, sending light spinning around the room. Stan wore his best white disco suit, tapping his foot to the beat and charging an exit fee for anyone who wanted to leave the party.

Outside, Dipper fidgeted at the ticket table. He had to put his plan into action.

"Step six: casual banter," he whispered to himself. He ducked under the table to look at his checklist. Then he sat back up and turned to Wendy.

"So, here's a casual question." His voice cracked. "What's your favorite type of snack food?"

"Oh man, I can't just pick one," Wendy replied.

"No way! Mine too!" Dipper blurted out.

Wendy looked confused. "Wait. What?"

"Uh, I mean, I mean . . ." Dipper coughed

nervously and ducked under the table again. "New topic! New topic!" he muttered to himself.

Inside, Mabel scanned the party for some possible new friends. She saw two right away: one girl had forks taped to the fingers on her right hand, and the other girl had a large lizard perched on her shoulder.

Mabel approached them. "Wow! You've got an animal on your body! I'm Mabel."

"Hi, I'm Grenda!" the girl with the lizard said in a deep voice. "This is Candy."

"Why do you have forks taped to your fingers?" Mabel asked Candy.

Candy smiled and dipped her fork hand into the popcorn bowl on Grenda's lap. When she pulled it out, she had a piece of popcorn on each fork. "Improvement of human being," she said, and she and Grenda laughed.

Mabel grinned. "I've found my people," she whispered.

From his DJ stand, Soos lowered the music.

He started reading aloud from his book:
"'Remember, dudes: whoever "party hardy-iest" gets the party crown. Most applause at the end of the night wins.'"

He held up the jeweled crown, which glittered under the disco lights. The girls gasped. It was beautiful!

Then a blond girl marched up to Soos's DJ stand. "Party crown? I'll take that, thank you very much!"

"Who's that?" Mabel asked her new friends.

"The most popular girl in town. Pacifica Northwest," Candy replied.

"I always feel bad about myself around her," Grenda said.

"Uh, I can't just *give* you the crown," Soos told Pacifica. "It's sort of a competition thing."

Pacifica sneered and took the mic from him. "Honestly, who's gonna compete against *me*?" she asked. She pointed at Candy and Grenda. "Fork girl? Lizard lady? Ha!"

Pacifica's friends laughed along with her.

"Hold me, Candy!" Grenda hugged her friend.

"Our kind isn't welcome here," Candy said sadly.

Mabel got a determined look on her face. She marched up to Soos. "Hey! I'll compete!" she said, and then she turned to Pacifica and smiled. "I'm Mabel."

"That sounds like a fat old lady's name," Pacifica said.

"I'll take that as a compliment," Mabel said, still smiling.

Pacifica's eyes narrowed. "May the best partier win."

"Nice meeting you!" Mabel said, waving cheerfully as Pacifica slowly danced backward. Then she lowered her voice. "She's going down."

The crowd clapped and cheered as Mabel and Pacifica got ready to see who could "party hardy-iest." The applause drifted outside to Dipper and Wendy.

"Wow, sounds like the party's getting nuts," Wendy said. She stood up and looked through the window. "I've gotta get in there. Cover for me?"

"Um, well, I..." Dipper stammered. This wasn't how the plan was supposed to go.

"Thanks, man!" Wendy said, and darted inside. Soon she was dancing under the disco lights.

Dipper couldn't stand it. He was supposed to be in there, dancing with Wendy! On the ticket table, he turned the OPEN side of the sign to the CLOSED side.

"I'll be back shortly," he told the kids in line. Then he felt something yank on his collar.

"What are you doing, kid?" Grunkle Stan barked, holding Dipper two feet off the ground while his legs dangled. "These suckers aren't gonna rip *themselves* off. You promised, remember?"

Dipper sighed. "Yeah."

Stan dropped him and stomped away. Dipper looked longingly through the window at the party room, where Wendy was still dancing.

"If only I could be two places at once," he said, and the party fliers flapped in the breeze next to him. They reminded him of the copier machine.

Two places at once. That was it! He kept up the CLOSED sign and quickly snuck into the Mystery Shack's old storage room. He lifted the lid off the copier, climbed onto the glass, and pressed the button.

"I wonder if this is a good idea." The copier

whirred and the eerie green light glowed through the glass. The machine scanned his body, and when it finished, he jumped off to see a Dipper-sized piece of paper slide from the copier.

It looked like a facedown picture of Dipper. Then color crept into the image and it came to life, rising off the floor. It turned to face Dipper, who gazed in awe at the copier clone he had created. It was like looking into a 3-D mirror.

"Whoa! I have a really big head!" said Dipper.

"**SO, UH,**" both Dippers said at the same time. Then they chuckled. "Sorry, you first. Stop copying me!"

Dipper and his clone laughed. The machine had made a copy that not only looked like Dipper but thought just like him, too. So

Dipper's clone was saying everything Dipper would say.

Dipper took a black marker and wrote a number 2 on the clone's hat. "I will call you Number Two," Dipper said.

"Definitely not. You know what name I've always wanted?" the clone asked.

Of course Dipper knew. He and the clone had the exact same mind.

"Tyrone!" Dipper and his clone said together.

"Okay, Tyrone, let's get down to business," Dipper said, remembering why he had copied himself in the first place. "I'm thinking you cover for me at the ticket stand while I ask Wendy to dance."

Tyrone nodded. "I know the plan, buddy!"

Dipper frowned. "Hey, we're not going to get jealous and turn on each other like the clones in the movies, are we?"

"Dipper, please. This is you you're talking about," Tyrone said. "Plus, you can always disintegrate me with water."

Dipper grinned. "Yeah!"

So Tyrone went outside to work the ticket stand while Dipper strolled up to Wendy on the dance floor.

"Great news, Wendy," he said. "I got somebody to cover the concessions for me."

Wendy turned to him, smiling. "That's awesome. You can hang out with me and Robbie. Robbie, you remember Dipper from the convenience store?"

A tall teen turned to face them. His black hair hung over his eyes, and he had an electric guitar strapped to his back. Behind him, a silver-and-red mountain bike leaned against the wall.

"Uh, no," Robbie said in a dull voice. Then he took the guitar from its case and played some licks on it. "Wendy, check out my new guitar."

Wendy's eyes lit up. "Whoa, cool!"

Dipper gasped in horror. Robbie was *not* in the plan! He could only imagine what would happen next, and a jealous fantasy flashed in his mind:

Wendy and Robbie were on the dance floor, dancing to a slow song.

"Robbie, you're a stupid, arrogant fraud, but kiss me anyway because you can play guitar!" Wendy said. "Oh, wait, I forgot something!"

Wendy walked across the dance floor and punched Dipper right in the gut.

She called out to Robbie, "Let's get married tonight!"

Dipper's cell phone roused him from his fantasy. It was Tyrone.

"Hey, buddy, it's me—you," he said. "I just had the same jealousy fantasy."

"We gotta get rid of Robbie if I ever want to dance with Wendy," Dipper said.

"Hey, Dipper! We're gonna go sit on the couch," said Wendy.

"Meet us when you're done." She and Robbie walked off the dance floor.

Dipper panicked. "Oh no! They're sitting on the couch! We gotta think of something quick!" he wailed into his phone. Then he noticed Robbie's bicycle. "I got an idea."

"I got the same one," said Tyrone, looking through the window. "But we're gonna need some help."

A couple of minutes later, they were both in the storage room, and a second clone popped out of the copier.

"And that's where you come in, Number Three," Dipper said after he explained the plan to the new clone.

"But what if Robbie catches me?" asked Number Three. "I'll be all alone."

"Okay, one more. One more clone," Dipper said. "This is a four-Dipper plan." He hopped up on the copier again and pressed the button. A puff of black smoke burst from the machine, and it made a grinding noise.

"Uh-oh! Paper jam," said Tyrone, going to the feeder. The paper coming out had Dipper's image on it, but it was all crinkled. Tyrone laid it on the floor and the image came to life. It looked like a crunched-up version of Dipper.

"Nyahh aaah eeek pfft!" Paper Jam Dipper screeched, jumping into Tyrone's arms.

"You're not going to make me partner up with *him*, are you?" Number Three asked Tyrone.

"Shhh. Don't be rude," Tyrone whispered as Paper Jam Dipper screeched and tugged on his lower lip like a poorly behaved monkey.

Dipper sighed. "Okay. Just one more clone."

Back on the dance floor, Mabel and Pacifica were battling it out to see who could party the hardy-iest. Pacifica stood in the spotlight, singing a pop song. The crowd clapped as she finished on a glass-shattering high note.

"I used to sing like that," Grenda said, "before my voice changed."

"Pacifica pulls ahead," Soos announced.

Pacifica handed Mabel the microphone. "Try and top that," she said. "Oh, and, Grenda, by the way, you sound like a professional wrestler."

Pacifica walked away, laughing, as Grenda balled her hands into fists. "I wanna put her in a headlock and make her feel pain!" she growled.

"It's not over till it's over, sisters," Mabel promised Candy and Grenda. "Watch this. Soos, get me the eighties-est, crowd-pleasing-est, rock-balladie-est song you got!"

Soos pressed some buttons, and the sounds of a 1980s rock ballad flowed from the speakers. Mabel took to the stage and started to sing.

"Don't start unbelieving! Never don't not feel your feelings!"

The crowd went crazy for the song, and Mabel ended with a body flip—and landed on her face.

"That was for you guys!" she yelled, and everyone whooped and cheered.

Just then, Dipper ran up and whispered

something in Soos's ear. Soos nodded and spoke into the microphone.

"Dudes, would the owner of a silver-and-red dirt bike please report outside? It is being stolen right now."

"Wait, what?" Robbie asked, and he looked out the window to see the backs of two guys who were riding off with his bike.

Little did he know they were two Dipper clones!

"Hey, come back here!" Robbie yelled, running outside.

"Oh, tough break," Dipper told Wendy, laughing nervously. "I wonder who those guys are that aren't me because I'm right here."

"Now we're gonna bring it down for a minute." Soos pressed some more buttons. "Ladies, dudes, now is the time."

A slow dance groove filled the room.

"Oh, snap! Love this song!" Wendy told Dipper.

Mabel ran up to her brother. "Hey, goofus, now's your chance to ask Wendy to dance! Come on! Go!" she whispered, giving him a push.

Dipper pulled his checklist from his pocket and studied it. Then he looked at Wendy, who was still sitting on the couch, swaying to the music. All he had to do was speak up and ask her.

"I, uh," he stammered, suddenly feeling sweaty. "I'll be right back."

He rushed to his room, where he found Tyrone waiting for him.

"Oh, I agree. You can't just go and dance with her!" Tyrone said.

"The dance floor is a minefield. A minefield, Tyrone!" Dipper wailed.

"What if there's a glitch in the sound system?" Tyrone asked.

"Stan might get in the way," Dipper said.

"Robbie might come back," added Tyrone.

"There's too many variables," he said, looking his clone in the eye. They were both thinking the same thing.

"We need help!"

CHAPTER FOUR

THE COPIER WHIRRED and whooshed
and glowed with green light as Dipper made five
more copies of himself! All eleven Dippers
headed up to Dipper's room and immediately got
to work on a new Wendy plan. (Well, maybe not
all ten clones contributed to the plan. Paper Jam

Dipper mostly drooled and made babbling noises.) They talked excitedly and wrote up new checklists of steps for Dipper to take.

"All right, Dippers! Gather 'round!" the real Dipper finally yelled, and nine of his clones lined up neatly in front of him. "Now's the time! You all clear on what to do?"

They all nodded and then headed back downstairs to set their plan into action.

First, Number Ten set out to distract Soos with a laser light.

"Hey, Soos, look! A glowing dot!" Number Ten cried, pointing to the wall behind Soos. Then he shone a green laser dot on the wall and moved it up and down.

"Oh man, I'm so glad I turned my head," Soos said. "That dot does not disappoint." He tried to catch the moving green light in his hands as if it were a firefly.

While Soos's back was turned, Number Ten slipped a special disc labeled WENDY MIX into the CD player. Number Five put a colored cell over the light shining onto the dance floor, casting a romantic pink glow everywhere. Number Seven pulled down the shades on the window. And Number Eight dangled a dollar in front of Stan on a fishing pole.

"Right, like I'm gonna fall for that," Stan said—and then he lunged at it. "Ahh! Give me that money!" he yelled, chasing it outside.

A bell rang in Dipper's room, signaling that the coast was clear.

"There's your cue," said Tyrone. "It's the perfect moment to ask Wendy to dance. Good luck, me!"

"I don't need luck. I have a plan!" Dipper said confidently, patting the folded checklist in his pocket. He ran downstairs, into the hallway... and then screamed! Wendy was standing in the hall—not down on the dance floor like she was supposed to be. Not like in the plan.

"Oh, hey, man. What's up?" Wendy said.

"Wh—what are you doing here?" Dipper asked her. "I mean, wouldn't you rather be out

on the dance floor? Uh, in like exactly forty-two seconds?"

"I'm just waiting in line for the bathroom," Wendy said.

Dipper quickly turned his back to her and looked at his checklist. "Um, okay. Small talk, small talk," he muttered to himself, starting to sweat.

"So, hey, let's say everyone at this party gets stuck on a desert island. Who do you think the leader would be?" Wendy asked him.

It was a great question, and Dipper knew it. But he was too nervous to answer it.

"I, uh . . ."

"I think I'd go with this lunatic," Wendy said, pointing down to the dance floor where a short guy was doing intense karate moves to the music.

Dipper laughed and hid his checklist. "I'd probably go for Stretch over there." He pointed to a really tall, really skinny guy. "Uh, because tall people can reach coconuts?"

Wendy laughed. "Speaking of tall, you wanna see something?" She took out her wallet and showed him a photo of three boys. She covered the last person in the photo with her finger. "Those are my three brothers, and I'm ... boop!" She lifted up her finger to reveal a super-tall skinny girl with pigtails and braces who towered over the boys. It was Wendy!

"Ha! You were a freak!" Dipper blurted out, and then quickly clapped his hand over his mouth. But Wendy wasn't insulted.

"Yup," she said, nodding.

"You know, kids used to make fun of my birthmark before I started hiding it all the time," Dipper said.

"Birthmark?" Wendy asked him.

"Uh, no, it's nothing," Dipper said nervously. "Why did I say that?" he muttered to himself.

"No way, dude!" Wendy said, her eyes gleaming. "Now you have to show me. Show me! Show me!"

Taking a deep breath, Dipper took off his hat and lifted the hair from his forehead. The birthmark looked exactly like . . .

"The Big Dipper!" Wendy cried out, amazed at the pattern of dots and lines that looked just like the constellation of stars in the sky. "That's how you got your nickname. I thought your parents just hated you or something." She smiled. "Hey, I guess we're both freaks!"

She handed Dipper a cup of soda, and they clinked cups. Then the bathroom door opened and Pacifica stomped out.

"Wait here?" Wendy asked Dipper.

"Of course!" Dipper replied as Wendy ducked inside.

Then Dipper heard footsteps behind him and turned to see Tyrone leading most of the clones into the hall.

"Hey! What are you doing up here?" Tyrone asked. "Number Ten has been distracting Soos for fifteen minutes. He's gonna get tired of that dot eventually."

"Never!" Soos yelled out from his DJ stand.

"You won't believe it, guys!" Dipper said excitedly. "I bumped into Wendy accidentally and things are actually going great."

"That's nice," Tyrone said, "but not the plan! Do we have to remind you?"

The clones started reading from their many checklists all at once.

"Stick to the plan!"

"Don't take any risks!"

"Oh man, you guys sound crazy!" Dipper realized. "Look, maybe we don't need the plan anymore, you know? Maybe I could just go talk to her like a normal person?"

Number Nine gasped.

"What?" asked Number Eight.

"You bite your tongue!" yelled Number Seven.

"If you're not gonna stick to the plan, maybe you shouldn't be the Dipper to dance with Wendy," said Number Five.

The other clones nodded. "Five. Number Five's on the ball."

"Guys, come on!" Dipper said. "We said we weren't gonna turn on each other."

"I think we all knew we were lying," Tyrone said, a dark expression crossing his face.

All of the clones converged on Dipper, pinning him down and grabbing him by the legs. Then they dragged him down the hallway.

"Aaaaaaaaah!" Dipper screamed.

CHAPTER FIVE

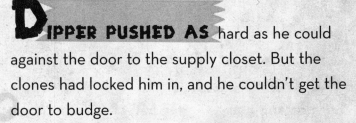

DIPPER PUSHED AS hard as he could against the door to the supply closet. But the clones had locked him in, and he couldn't get the door to budge.

"No, wait!" he yelled, panicked. "I can't breathe in here."

"Yeah, you can!" Tyrone said through the door. "Plus, there's snacks and a coloring book in there for you."

Dipper grunted, frustrated, and then picked up a snack pack of cheese and crackers. Those other Dippers sure knew him well.

Out in the hall, Tyrone addressed the other clones. "Okay, so now that original Dipper, or 'Dipper Classic,' is no longer fit for it, I nominate myself to dance with Wendy instead. I've been around the longest, so it should be me, right? I mean, logically. Logically, guys."

"Fair point, fair point," said Number Ten. "Counterpoint: maybe I should get to dance with Wendy because I've been around her the least."

"That makes, like, zero sense," said Number Five.

Number Ten turned to him, angry. "You make zero sense!" he yelled, shoving him.

Number Five shoved him back. "Watch it!"

"Don't shove, people!" said Number Six.

"*Blaaarf!*" added Paper Jam Dipper.

Tyrone strolled up to him, holding a snack pack. "Hey, you want some cheese and crackers, buddy?"

"*Aiiiieeeek!*" replied the crumpled-up clone.

Tyrone tried to fit a cracker into Paper Jam Dipper's mouth and it fell to the floor.

"Yikes." Suddenly, something dawned on Tyrone. "Hey, guys, what would you do if you were trapped in a closet?"

"Break out!" the other clones answered, and then they all turned at once. The closet door was open. Dipper had escaped!

Dipper ran downstairs as fast as he could. He reached the hall overlooking the dance floor.

"Wen—!" he cried out, but Tyrone clapped a hand over his mouth and pulled him away from the railing.

"Come on, man, give it up," Tyrone said. "You're overpowered."

"Hold on, guys," Dipper said. "Think about it! We're exact equals, mentally and physically. If we start fighting, it'll just go on for infinity."

Tyrone nodded. "It's true when you think about it."

The clones began to chatter. What Dipper said made sense.

"Maybe we should just give up," said Number Nine.

Then Dipper punched Tyrone in the jaw.

"Clone fight!" yelled Number Nine.

The clones turned on each other, punching and kicking.

Number Five slapped Dipper's face again and again. "Hey, quit hitting myself! Quit hitting myself!" taunted Number Five. Then Number Six came flying out of nowhere and tackled him. Clones fought left and right, slapping each other in the stomachs and twisting each other's arms.

Dipper took advantage of the chaos and slowly walked off. Number Ten saw him.

"Hey, Classic Dipper's getting away!" he yelled.

But Dipper had a plan. He had taped a "7" to the front of his hat.

"No, friends, it's me. Number Seven," he said, pointing to the hat.

"That's not me, guys. That's not me!" said Number Seven, and just then, the "7" fell off of Dipper's hat.

"Get him!" shouted Number Nine.

"Stay back! Stay back!" Dipper said warningly. He pulled the only weapon he had out of his pocket—a party popper.

Poof! He pulled the tab and confetti streamed from the popper. Which was pretty lame—except that the smoke from the popper wafted up to the fire sprinklers on the ceiling. Water rained down on eight of the clones, melting them.

"Huh. How about that," Dipper muttered as the sprinkler shut off. Then he heard a familiar voice behind him, and turned.

Tyrone pointed at him accusingly. "You!"

"Uh-oh," Dipper said.

CHAPTER SIX

BACK ON THE dance floor, the contest to
see who could party the hardy-iest was in full
swing. Mabel did the Worm, while the crowd
that had gathered around her cheered and
clapped.

"One more song, dudes," Soos announced. "And then it's time for the bestowing of the party crown. It's gonna be the . . ."

He pressed a button, and the sound of a bomb exploding reverberated. Soos smiled. "Nailed it!"

Mabel walked up to Pacifica. "Pacifica, I just want to say that whoever wins, it's been a super-fun party." She held out her hand.

Pacifica did not shake her hand. "Aw, it thinks it's gonna win," she said meanly. Then she cupped her hand around her ear. "Hey, did you hear that? People clapping for the weird girl? Yeah, me neither."

She walked away, but Mabel didn't lose her smile. She was having fun—and Pacifica wasn't going to ruin it!

Upstairs, Tyrone had Dipper in a headlock.

"Say it! Say I can dance with Wendy!" said Tyrone.

"Never!" Dipper grunted, breaking free and putting the headlock on Tyrone instead.

But both boys froze when they heard Wendy's laugh floating up from the dance floor.

"Wendy?" they asked at once, and both moved to the railing to investigate.

Robbie had returned! He and Wendy were tucked in a corner, talking and laughing. Dipper and Tyrone sighed.

"We blew it, man!" they said together. Then they sank to the floor in defeat.

"I don't know, do you wanna go and grab a couple of sodas or something?" Tyrone asked.

As the two boys headed downstairs, Soos was riling up the crowd on the dance floor. He stood on the stage, flanked by Mabel and Pacifica.

"Let the party-crown voting commence!" he announced.

"Good luck, Mabel," Pacifica said, peering around Soos's belly. Then her eyes narrowed. She clearly didn't mean it.

"Applaud to vote for Mabel!" Soos yelled.

Lots of people applauded, including Stan and Mabel's new friends, Candy and Grenda.

"Yeah, go, Mabel!" Grenda bellowed.

"Let's check the applause-o-meter," Soos said, raising his right arm like it was the arm on a real applause-measuring machine. His arm stopped straight up in the air. "Pretty good!"

Mabel grinned.

"And your next contestant: Pacifica!" Soos announced.

At first, only Pacifica's friends clapped. Then Pacifica glared at the other kids and they

nervously started applauding, too. Soos's left arm went up, up—and stopped straight up in the air, even with his right arm.

"Uh-oh. A tie? This has, like, never happened before," Soos said.

Pacifica frowned. She wasn't used to losing, or tying—just winning. But she got an idea. She marched over to Old Man McGuckett, who was dozing on some folding chairs. She dangled a dollar in front of his face. Sniffing the air, he woke up and grabbed it. Then he clapped with glee.

Soos's left arm started to move. The applause put Pacifica over the top!

"Ladies and gentlemen, we have a winner," Soos said sadly. "The winner of the contest is Pacifica Northwest."

Soos put the crown on her head. "Thank you, everyone!" she said, beaming at the crowd. "Everyone come to the after-party at my parents' boat! Woo-hoo!"

A bunch of the kids in the crowd picked up Pacifica. They streamed out of the Mystery Shack, chanting, "Pacifica! Pacifica! Pacifica!"

Mabel looked sad. "Sorry I let you guys down," she told Candy and Grenda, who had stayed behind. "I understand if you want to leave."

"But then we would miss the sleepover," Candy said with a grin.

Mabel was puzzled. "The *what*?"

"We wanna call our moms and sleep over here with you. You're, like, a total rock star!" said Grenda.

Candy took the latest issue of *Cool Dudes* out of her backpack. "I have magazine boys!"

Mabel's face lit up. "Really? You guys!"

"Maybe we don't have as many friends as Pacifica, but we have each other," Candy said. "And that is pretty good, I think."

"Soos!" Mabel called out. "Play another song. This thing's going all night!"

"Way ahead of you, hambone," Soos replied, sliding a record onto the turntable. The music started, and Mabel and her new friends started to dance.

Dipper and his clone didn't feel much like dancing. They sat on the roof, gazing at the stars. They each popped open a can of Pitt Cola.

"You think we really even have a chance with Wendy?" Dipper asked Tyrone. "I mean, she's fifteen, we're twelve. . . ."

"I don't know, man," Tyrone replied. "I hope so, but we're making zero progress the way we're doing it. The only good conversation you had with her was when you didn't do any of that list stuff."

Dipper nodded. "I know. Mabel was right. I do get in my own way."

"Literally!" they said in unison.

The two boys clinked soda cans, and each took a sip. Then a look of horror came over Tyrone's face.

"Oh boy! Don't look now," he said, gazing down at his stomach, which was beginning to ripple. The soda was dissolving him from the inside!

"Tyrone!" cried Dipper.

"It's okay, dude. I had a good run," Tyrone said as he melted. "Remember what we talked about!"

"Of course!" said Dipper.

Tyrone's body was just a puddle. Only his head remained.

"Hey, and quit being such a wimp around Wendy," he said as his head started to dissolve. "For my sake!" And with that, Tyrone was no more.

Dipper fell to his knees. "Tyrone! You were the only one who understood."

With a sigh, Dipper climbed down from the roof. He looked through the window into the Mystery Shack. Mabel and two girls were dancing, and Wendy stood against the wall, nodding her head to the music.

Dipper took out his checklist. If he followed the plan, maybe he could . . .

Rrrrrrrrip! He tore the list in half and stepped inside the shack.

From now on, there would be no more plans for trying to impress Wendy. It would be just Dipper—the original Dipper—being himself.

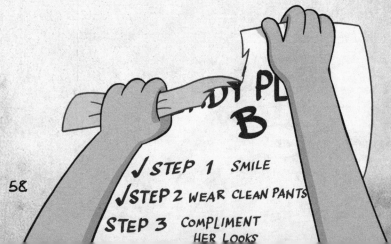

...DY PL
B

✓ STEP 1 SMILE
✓ STEP 2 WEAR CLEAN PANTS
STEP 3 COMPLIMENT
         HER LOOKS

CHAPTER ONE

STAN WAS ALWAYS looking for new ways to make money. One day, he tested out one of his new plans on a group of visitors who had just received a tour of the shack.

"For tonight's final illusion, we have the Incredible Sack of Mystery!" Stan dangled a burlap sack in front of them. "When you put your money in, it mysteriously disappears!"

The tourists happily obeyed.

"Oh, of course!" said one man.

"That makes perfect sense!" said another, as he dropped some bills into the sack.

Stan grinned. This new plan was working out even better than he'd hoped.

Inside the shack, Dipper, Mabel, and Soos were watching their favorite new show on TV— *Tiger Fist*—about a tiger with a human arm.

"All right!" Mabel cheered.

Then a commercial came on. It opened with a pair of hands releasing doves into the sky.

"Are you completely miserable?" a voice with a Southern accent asked. "Then you need to meet . . . Gideon!"

An outline of a person with a big question mark inside it appeared on the screen.

GIDEON

"Gideon," a gentle voice on the TV whispered.

Mabel thought out loud. "What makes him so special?"

"He's a psychic!" said the announcer. "So don't waste your time with other so-called 'Men of Mystery.'"

The next image showed Stan, in his underwear, coming out of the outhouse with toilet paper stuck to his slipper. The word FRAUD in large letters was stamped over him.

"Learn about tomorrow, tonight!" the announcer said as a picture of a tent appeared. "At Gideon's Tent of Telepathy!"

"Wow! I'm getting all curious-y inside," Mabel said.

Stan stomped in. "Don't get too curious-y," he growled. "Ever since that monster, Gideon, rolled into town, I've had nothing but trouble." It wasn't just the commercial that bothered him. Gideon was driving around town in a fancy RV, drawing crowds away from the Mystery Shack—and cutting into Stan's profits.

"Well, is he really psychic?" Mabel asked.

"I think we should go and find out," said Dipper.

"Never!" Stan grumbled. "You're forbidden from patronizing the competition! No one that lives under my roof is allowed under that Gideon's roof!"

Dipper looked at Mabel. "Do tents have roofs?"

She grinned. "I think we just found our loophole." Then Mabel pulled out a string that had a loop on one end. "Literally! Mwop-mwop!" she said, amused by her own terrible joke.

"So come on down soon, folks," said the announcer in an ominous voice. "Gideon is expecting ya."

That night, Dipper, Mabel, and Soos made their way to Gideon's tent. A mysterious symbol of a star with an eye in the middle topped the tent. Curious people streamed in, past a man in a Hawaiian shirt and straw hat who was holding a sack with the same symbol on it. His name tag read BUDDY.

"Step right up there, folks!" he said with the same Southern accent as the announcer in the commercial. "Put your money in Gideon's Psychic Sack! Only one thin dime."

Dipper, Mabel, and Soos took seats on one of the wood benches inside. Mabel munched on a sack of popcorn. Then the lights in the tent dimmed, and the audience hushed.

"It's starting, it's starting!" Mabel whispered excitedly.

"Let's see what this 'monster' looks like," Dipper said.

The curtain on the rickety wood stage in front of them opened—to reveal a short boy with a big white pompadour hairdo. Freckles dotted his chubby cheeks, and he wore a powderblue suit and a cape with the eye symbol on it. A green stone glimmered in the bolo he wore around his neck.

"Hello, America. My name is Lil' Gideon!" he announced to the cheers of the crowd. He clapped his hands, and doves flew out of his hair.

"*That's* Stan's mortal enemy?" Dipper wondered.

"But he's so widdle!" Mabel said.

"Ladies and gentlemen, it is such a gift to have you here tonight," Gideon said in a smooth drawl. "Such a gift." He pressed his hands together. "I have a vision. I predict you will soon all say, 'Awww.'"

He turned around, and then turned back with his eyes wide and cute like a kitten's.

"Awwwwwww!" the audience said.

Mabel's eyes grew wide. "It came true!"

Dipper shrugged. "What? I'm not impressed."

"You're impressed," Mabel said.

"Hit it, Dad!" Gideon called out, and the man in the straw hat started to play an electric piano. Gideon began to sing.

> *"Oh, I can see,*
> *What others can't see!*
> *It ain't some sideshow trick,*
> *It's an innate ability.*
> *Where others are blind,*
> *I am future-ly inclined,*
> *And you too could see*
> *If you wuz widdle ol' me!"*

Gideon waved his hands. "Come on, everybody, rise up! I want y'all to keep it going!"

Everyone got to their feet—even Dipper who had no intention of standing up at all.

"How did he—" Dipper said.

"Keep it going!" Gideon yelled. He pointed to an elderly woman. She had two cats on her lap.

"You wish your son would call you more," he sang.

She shook her fist. "I'm leaving everything to my cats."

One cat screeched as if it agreed with her.

"*I sense that you've been here before!*" He pointed at Sheriff Blubs.

The sheriff looked down at his arms filled with Gideon souvenirs. "Oh, what gave that away?"

Then Gideon sang to Mabel, who wore a sweater with MABEL written on it in rainbow letters.

"*I'll read your mind, if I'm able.*
Something tells me you're named Mabel!"

Mabel gasped. "How'd he do that?"

Gideon climbed back onto the stage. "*So welcome all ye, to the Tent of Telepathy. And thanks for visiting . . .*" He winked. "*Widdle ol' me!*"

Blue flames burst up on either side of him, and a neon sign blazing GIDEON dropped down from the ceiling.

Gideon panted, puffed, and pulled out a water bottle. He took a long sip. "Oh my goodness! Thank you! You people are the real miracles!"

"Whoo! Yeah!" Mabel cheered along with the crowd.

But Dipper wasn't impressed. "Man, that kid's a bigger fraud than Stan!" he said as they left the tent. "No wonder our uncle's jealous."

"Oh, come on, his dance moves were adorable!" Mabel said. "And did you see his hair? It was like, *whoosh!*"

Dipper shook his head. "You're too easily impressed."

"Yeah, yeah!" Mabel said with a laugh.

Gideon was cute and a lot of fun, but Mabel thought Dipper was probably right. Grunkle Stan was totally wrong about Gideon being a monster.

Behind them, Gideon peeked at Mabel from behind the flaps of the tent . . . and his cute widdle ol' eyes narrowed menacingly.

CHAPTER TWO

THE NEXT DAY, Mabel ran up to Dipper in the Mystery Shack holding a hot-pink glue gun. Her face was dotted with plastic blue, green, and pink jewels.

"Check it out, Dipper! I successfully bedazzled my face!" she announced. *Blink.* Jewels popped

off her eyelids. She
cringed. "Ow."
Dipper
shook
his head.
"Is that . . .
permanent?"

"I'm unappreciated in my time," said Mabel.
Then the doorbell rang.

"Somebody answer that door!" yelled Stan.

"I'll get it!" Mabel said, quickly brushing the
gems off her face. When she opened the door,
Gideon was standing there.

"Howdy," he said.

"It's widdle ol' you!" Mabel said excitedly.

"Yeah, my song's quite catchy," Gideon said
apologetically. "I, I know we haven't formally met,
but after yesterday's performance I just couldn't
get your laugh out of my head."

"You mean this one?" Mabel asked. Then she
let out a laugh that sounded like a baby seal
asking for fish. "Ah ha ha ha ha ha!"

"Oh, what a delight," Gideon said, beaming. "When I saw you in the audience, I said to myself, 'Now there's a kindred spirit. Someone who appreciates the sparkly things in life.'"

"That's totally me!" Mabel said. "Ha ha ha ha . . . *hork*," she laughed, choking up gems that sprayed Gideon and stuck fashionably to his lapel.

Gideon looked down at his sparkling lapel with admiration. "Enchanting. Utterly enchanting," whispered a smitten Gideon.

"Who's at the door?" boomed Stan from inside.

"No one, Grunkle Stan!" Mabel quickly lied.

"I appreciate your discretion," Gideon said. "That Stan's no fan of mine. I don't know how a lemon so sour could be related to a peach so sweet!"

He chuckled, and Mabel blushed. "Gideon!"

"What do you say we step away from here, and chat a bit more? Perhaps in my dressing room?" Gideon asked.

Mabel's eyes widened. "Makeovers! Yahoo!"
she cheered, poking Gideon's chubby belly.

"Eh, ha ha . . . ow," Gideon whispered to
himself.

They headed to Gideon's dressing room,
which was filled with dozens of glittery outfits
and accessories.

"Do you see something you like?" Gideon
asked. Then he looked at her and lowered his
voice. "'Cause I do."

But if Gideon was hinting that he liked Mabel, she was totally oblivious. She just thought he was a kindred spirit. They tried on outfits and then went to get their hair, makeup, and nails done. When Mabel got back to the Mystery Shack, she wiggled her fake nails in front of her brother's face.

"Whoa, where have you been?" Dipper asked her. "And what's going on with those fingernails? You look like a wolverine."

"I know, right?" She growled. "I was hanging out with my new pal, Gideon! He is one dapper little man!"

"Mabel, I don't trust anyone whose hair is bigger than their head," Dipper said.

"Oh, leave him alone!" Mabel said. "You never want to do girly stuff with me." She pointed at him. "You and Soos get to do boy stuff all the time."

"What do you mean?" Dipper said.

Then Soos ran in holding a pack of hot dogs.

"Hey, dude, you ready to blow up these hot dogs in the microwave, one at a time?"

"Am I?" Dipper cheered, and ran after him.

So Dipper didn't argue when Mabel hung out with Gideon again the next day. She and Gideon had climbed up to the roof of the factory that made all the Gideon souvenirs.

"Whoa! The view from your family's factory is nuts!" Mabel said. "Good thing we both brought our . . ."

"Opera glasses!" Mabel and Gideon said together, laughing.

Then they looked out over the trees and homes of Gravity Falls sprawled far below them.

"Mabel, when I'm up here, looking down on all of them little ol' people, I feel like I'm king of all I survey." A dark look crossed his face, but it cleared before Mabel could see it. "I guess that makes you my queen."

"What?" Mabel asked with a chuckle. "You are being so nice to me right now. Quit it!" She gave him a playful punch to the gut.

"I can't quit it," Gideon said smoothly. "I am speaking from the heart."

"From the where, now?" Mabel asked, eyes shifting.

"Mabel, I've never felt this close with anyone. So, so close." He reached out to stroke her hair twice, and she pushed his hand away twice.

"Hey, look, Gideon, I am . . . I like you a lot, but let's just be friends," Mabel said nervously. Mabel sometimes dreamed of having a boyfriend, but deep down she knew she was too young for one. And besides, she didn't like Gideon that way.

"At least just give me a chance," Gideon said. "Mabel, will you do me the honor of going on a date with me?"

"A playdate?" Mabel asked.

Gideon shook his head.

"A shopping date?" she asked hopefully.

"Uh-uh. It'll be just one little ol' date. I swear on my lucky bolo tie," he said, grasping the green stone around his neck. Then his eyes got all big and kitteny again. It was hard for Mabel to say no.

"Um . . . okay then, I guess," she said reluctantly.

Gideon smiled broadly. "Mabel Pines, you have made me the happiest boy in the world!" He enveloped Mabel in a hug.

After a few seconds, Mabel said, "Are you sniffing my hair?"

CHAPTER THREE

LATER ON at the Mystery Shack, Mabel and Dipper were playing video games. "It's not a date-date," Mabel explained to Dipper. "It's just, you know, I didn't want to hurt his feelings, and so I figured I'd throw him a bone."

"Mabel, guys don't work that way!" her brother told her. "He's gonna fall in love with you!"

Mabel laughed. "Yeah, right. I'm not *that* lovable."

"Okay, we agree on something here," Dipper said.

The doorbell rang, and Mabel went to get it. When she opened the door, a horse stepped into the shack! Mabel screamed and jumped back. Gideon was riding the horse, and wearing a powder-blue ten-gallon hat to match his suit.

"A night of enchantment awaits, my lady!" he said, holding out his hand for her.

"Oh boy," Mabel said under her breath. Something told her this was going to be way more than a "little ol' date."

Gideon took her to the fanciest restaurant in Gravity Falls. They sat in a big blue private booth.

"I can't believe they let us bring a horse in here," Mabel remarked, watching the horse drink out of the restaurant's decorative fountain.

"Well, people have a hard time saying no to me," Gideon explained. He leaned back and propped his feet up on the table.

A waiter with a long mustache approached. "Ah, Mr. Gideon, the feet on the table. An excellent choice!" he said in a French accent.

Gideon frowned. "Jean-Luc, what did we discuss about eye contact?"

The waiter backed away, looking into space. "Yes, yes! Very good!"

Mabel stared at the place setting in front of her. "I've never seen so many forks!" She lifted her drinking glass. "And water with bubbles in it! Ooh, la la! *Oui Oui!*"

Gideon cleared his throat. *"Parlez-vouz Français?"*

"I have no idea what you're saying," Mabel said blankly.

Back at the Mystery Shack, Stan was comfortably reading a newspaper in his underwear—until a picture on page six stopped him cold. He marched up to the cash register where Soos, Dipper, and Wendy were hanging out.

"Hey, hey! What the Jekyll is Mabel doing in the paper next to that greasy pickpocket Gideon?" he barked, pointing to the article. It showed Mabel and Gideon walking down the street, with the headline LIL' GIDEON'S LIL' GIRLFRIEND?

"Oh, yeah, it's like a big deal," Wendy said, scrolling through news updates on her phone.

"Everybody's talking about Gideon and Mabel's big date tonight."

Stan's face turned red. "What? That little shyster is dating my great-niece?"

"I wonder what the new name will be for the power couple," Soos said. "Mabideon? Gideabel?" Then he gasped. "May-Gid-Bel-Eon!"

"I didn't know!" Dipper told Stan. "I didn't hear about it! And plus, I told her not to!"

Stan rushed off and quickly changed into his suit.

"Yeah, well, it ends tonight," Stan said firmly, stomping toward the front door. "I'm going right down to that little skunk's house. This is going to stop right now!"

CHAPTER FOUR

MINUTES LATER, Stan came to a
screeching stop in front of the house where
Gideon and his father, Buddy Gleeful, lived. The
white-shingled house had an iron fence around it.
A billboard on the fence read HOME OF LIL'
GIDEON! LIKE FROM TV!

Stan swung open the gate and stomped down the walk, past a stone statue of Gideon with wings like a cupid. A flowery sign that said PARDON THIS GARDEN hung from the front door. Stan banged on the door as hard as he could.

"Gideon, you little punk! Open up!" He stopped to read the sign. "I will pardon nothing!" he yelled, and swatted the sign off the door.

Buddy Gleeful answered, his massive body taking up the doorframe. "Why, Stanford Pines! What a delight!"

"Out of the way, Bud," Stan said, pushing him aside. "I'm looking for Gideon."

Buddy smiled widely. "Well, I haven't seen the boy around, but since you're here, you simply must come in for coffee!" He put an arm around Stan and ushered him inside.

"B—but, I came—" he said, but Buddy placed a hand on his shoulder.

"Ah, it's imported! All the way from Colombia!"

Stan brightened. "Wow, I went to jail there

once!" he said, impressed. After all, when had he ever turned down a free cup of coffee?

He followed Buddy inside the living room, with its overstuffed lavender couch, recliner, and flowery rug.

"Some digs you got here," Stan said, looking around. Then he stopped in front of a sad clown painting on the wall and whistled in appreciation. "Wow! This is beautiful." Then he plopped down on the soft couch.

Buddy nervously cleared his throat. "Now, I hear your niece and Gideon are—well, they're singing in harmony, so to speak," Buddy said with a chuckle, as he placed a steaming mug on the coffee table.

"Uh, yeah! And I'm against it." Stan knocked a couch pillow onto the floor.

"No, no, no! I see it as a fantastic business opportunity! The Mystery Shack and the Tent of Telepathy!" Buddy said, helping Stan up and walking him across the room. "We've been at each other's throats for far too long." Upon seeing a photo of Stan pinned to a dartboard, Buddy snatched it off and said, "Let me get that." He tossed it over his shoulder and continued walking. "This is our big chance to brush aside our rivalry, and pool our collective profits, you see."

The word "profits" caught Stan's attention. "I'm listening."

Back at the restaurant, Mabel and Gideon were finishing their fancy dinner. Gideon wiped his face with his napkin. Mabel looked down at the still-alive lobster on her plate. She couldn't bear to have them cook it for her.

"Mabel, tonight's date was a complete success!" Gideon announced. "And tomorrow's date promises to top this one in every way!"

"Whoa, whoa!" Mabel said. "You said just one date! And this was it!" And for Mabel, it hadn't been a success at all. Gideon had talked about himself the whole time. It was rude to bring a horse into a restaurant, and who ate cute lobsters, anyway?

Gideon held out his arm. "Hark! What a surprise! A red-crested South American rainbow macaw!"

An enormous bird bigger than Gideon's head flew to their table and landed on Gideon's outstretched arm. Gideon counted down. Then the bird began to squawk out a message, one word at a time.

"Mabel. Will. You. Accompany. Gideon. To. The. Ballroom. Dance. This. Thurbday. Er, Thursday."

Now everybody in the restaurant was looking at them.

"Aw, so adorable!" said one woman, as the macaw flew away.

The chef smiled at them from the kitchen. "Gideon's got a girlfriend!"

"They're expecting us," Gideon whispered. "Please say you'll go?"

"Awww," everyone said as they gathered around the table.

Mabel did not want to say yes. Not one little bit.

"Gideon, I'm sorry, but I'm gonna have to say—"

Sheriff Blubs interrupted her. "I'm on the edge of my seat!"

"This is gonna be adorable," said a skinny biker.

"If she says no, I'll die from sadness!" wailed an old lady.

A doctor spoke up from behind her. "I can verify that that will indeed happen."

Everyone at the restaurant cheered and hollered for Mabel.

Mabel sighed. She wanted to say no. But how could she when everyone wanted her to say yes?

When Mabel returned to the Mystery Shack, Dipper was reading from Journal #3. Mabel walked in with the lobster from the restaurant.

"Hey, how'd it go?" Dipper asked her.

"I don't know," Mabel said with a sigh. "I have a lobster now." She carefully dropped the lobster into the big fish tank and watched it sink.

"Well, at least it's over and you won't ever have to go out with him again," Dipper said, waiting for a "yes" from his sister. But he didn't get one. "Mabel? It's over, right?"

Mabel threw up her hands. "Blargh! He asked me out again and I didn't know how to say no!"

"Like this," Dipper said. "No."

"It's not that easy, Dipper!" Mabel said. "And I do like Gideon. As a friend slash little sister! So I didn't want to hurt his feelings!" She sat in a chair across from Dipper. "I just need to get things back to where they used to be. You know, friends!"

But Gideon had other ideas. Mabel went to the dance with him, like she had promised, but Gideon insisted that they take a boat ride on the Gravity Falls Lake afterward. Old Man McGuckett rowed the boat while they glided across the moonlit water.

"Boatin' at night! Boatin' at night!" McGuckett screamed to no one in particular.

Mabel laughed nervously as she looked in Gideon's eyes. "You know I thought dancing was going to be the end of the evening, right?"

Gideon grabbed her hands. "Don't you want this evening to last, my sweet?"

Mabel quickly pulled her hands away. "No! I mean, yes. I mean, I'm always happy to hang out with a friend. Buddy. Pal. Chum. Other word for friend."

"Pal?" Old Man McGuckett said.

"I already said pal. Uh, mate?" Mabel said.

"How about . . . soul mate?" Gideon asked as he leaned close to her. Fireworks exploded above them, spelling out MABEL inside a pink heart.

"Well, you can't say no to that!" said Old Man McGuckett.

And Mabel couldn't say no. Gideon locked her into another date before he brought her back to the shack.

Inside, she nervously paced back and forth across the floor.

"He's so nice, but I can't keep doing this, but I can't break his heart. Argh! I have no way out!" she said to herself, feeling frantic.

Dipper poked his head into the living room. "What in the heck happened on that date?"

"I don't know!" Mabel wailed. "I was in the friend zone. And then, before I knew what was happening, he pulled me into the romance zone. It was like quicksand!" She grabbed Dipper's shoulders. "Chubby quicksand!"

Dipper hated to see his sister freaking out like this. "Mabel, come on. It's not like you're going to have to marry Gideon."

Then Stan burst into the room. "Great news, Mabel! You have to marry Gideon!"

CHAPTER FIVE

MABEL'S MOUTH dropped open.
"What?"

"It's all part of my long-term deal with Buddy
Gleeful!" Stan said. "There's a lot of cash tied up
in this thing. Plus, I got this shirt."

He looked down at the T-shirt he was wearing.

It read TEAM GIDEON. The tight shirt hugged his jiggly belly.

"Ugh, am I fat," Stan said.

Mabel screamed and ran out of the room.

"Bodies change, honey!" he called after her. "Bodies change."

Dipper followed Mabel up the stairs to their attic bedroom. At first, he didn't see Mabel. But then he noticed her hiding in the corner, rocking back and forth, with the collar of her sweater pulled up to cover her entire head.

"Oh no," Dipper said. "Mabel?"

"Mabel's not here. She's in Sweater Town," she said miserably.

"Are you gonna come out of Sweater Town?" Dipper asked.

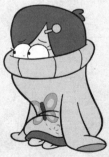

Mabel just moaned and shook her head.

"All right. Enough is enough! If you can't break up with Gideon, then I'll do it for you."

Mabel poked her head out of the sweater. "You will?" Mabel asked.

Dipper nodded.

Then she hugged her brother and gave him playful punches. "Oh, thank you, thank you, thank you, thank you, thank you!"

Mabel knew they could find Gideon at The Club, where the rich people in Gravity Falls hung out. She waited outside while Dipper went in to talk to Gideon. He found Gideon sitting at a table by himself.

"Oh, Dipper Pines, how are you?" Gideon asked, placing down his enormous menu. "You look good, you look good."

"Thanks, you, uh—" But Dipper couldn't think of anything nice to say. He simply scratched his head. "Look, Gideon, we've gotta talk. Mabel isn't joining you tonight. She, uh, doesn't want to see you anymore." He chuckled nervously. "She's, uh, she's kind of weirded out by you. No offense!"

Gideon's eyes narrowed. "So what you're saying is, you've come between us," he said through clenched teeth. His eye twitched.

Dipper didn't like the look on his face. "You're not gonna, like, freak out or anything, are ya?"

"Of course not!" Gideon changed his tune and gave a gentle laugh. "These things happen. Bygones, you know."

Dipper nodded. "So okay, cool. Well then, again, sorry, man, but, uh, thumbs-up, right?"

Dipper forced a smile and gave Gideon a thumbs-up. Then he quickly backed up and went outside, where Mabel was nervously waiting for him.

"How did it go? Was he mad? Did he try to read your mind with his psychic powers?" she asked.

"Don't worry, Mabel, he's just a kid," Dipper assured her. "He doesn't have any powers."

Over at Gideon's house, Gideon was fuming. Up in his bedroom, he stared at his reflection in his lighted makeup mirror.

"Dipper Pines, you don't know what you've done!" he growled angrily. He placed his hand on the stone around his neck and an eerie green glow emitted from it.

Pop! Pop! Pop! The light bulbs around the mirror exploded one by one. His dresser, nightstand, and bed levitated off the floor.

"You've just made the biggest mistake of your life!" Gideon growled, thinking of Dipper. He angrily pointed at his floating dresser.

Crash! It fell to the floor, breaking into pieces.

His father pushed open the door. "Gideon Charles Gleeful! Clean up your room this instant!"

Gideon spun around, his eyes blazing. He pointed a stubby finger at his father. "I can buy and sell you, old man!"

Buddy shrugged. "Fair enough." Then he backed out of the room.

But Dipper and Mabel had no idea how angry Gideon was—or that he really had magic powers. Back at the Mystery Shack, they were hanging out, taking turns punching the pillow that Soos had stuck under his T-shirt.

"I'm so glad everything's back to normal," Mabel said, relieved.

Then the phone rang, and Dipper picked it up.

"Toby Determined, *Gravity Falls Gossiper*," said the voice on the other end.

"Oh, hey, man! It's Dipper," Dipper said.

"We want to interview you about whether

you've seen anything unusual in this here town since you've arrived," the reporter said.

"Oh, finally!" Dipper said. "I thought nobody would ever ask! I have notes and theories."

Dipper wrote down the address that Toby gave him. "Tonight? Got it."

Dipper was excited. He had been taking lots of notes about every strange thing he'd seen in Gravity Falls since he arrived this summer. It would be great to share his stories with the world.

It didn't even occur to him that it might be a trap. That Gideon had bribed Toby to get Dipper exactly where he wanted him—alone, and on Gideon's turf.

That night, Dipper rode his bicycle to the address Toby had given him—412 Gopher Road. He found himself at a factory on top of a tall cliff that overlooked the whole town. Dipper stepped through the open bay and cautiously called into the darkness. "Hello?"

The door slammed shut behind him. He tried

to open it, slamming his fist against it, but it was locked. He spun around as the lights came on. A desk chair swiveled around to reveal Gideon seated in it. He patted a Lil' Gideon doll on his lap. It looked just like a mini version of himself.

"Hello, friend," said Gideon in a sweet voice.

Dipper was annoyed. "Gideon?"

"Dipper Pines, how long have you been living in this town?" Gideon asked. "A week? Two? You like it here? Enjoy the scenery?"

"What do you want from me, man?" Dipper asked.

"Listen carefully, boy," Gideon said, his voice darkening. "This town has secrets you couldn't begin to comprehend."

"Is this about Mabel?" Dipper asked. "I told you, she's not into you!"

"Liar!" Gideon snapped. He jumped out of his chair and stomped toward Dipper. "You turned her against me. She was my peach dumpling!"

Gideon's face flushed with anger. The stone

on his bolo tie started to glow as he placed a hand on it.

"Uh, are you okay, man?" Dipper asked.

Blue-green light from the stone surrounded Dipper. He gasped as the light lifted him off the floor. Then it tossed him backward, crashing him into a stack of boxes of Lil' Gideon dolls.

"Howdy!" one of the dolls squeaked.

Gideon flashed a sinister grin. "Reading minds isn't all I can do."

Dipper couldn't believe his eyes. "B—but— you're a fake!" But he wasn't so sure anymore.

"Oh, tell me, Dipper, is this fake?" Gideon placed a hand on his stone.

He raised his other hand and the boxes in the factory started opening up. Dipper gasped as Gideon dolls, clocks, and mugs floated up into the air, suspended by blue light!

CHAPTER SIX

WHILE DIPPER was caught in Gideon's clutches, Mabel sat on the porch of the Mystery Shack, chewing a strand of her hair. At first, she was glad that Dipper was taking care of her Gideon problem for her. But then she started to feel bad. Deep down, she knew that she should be the one to do it.

Wendy sat down beside her. "How's that hair tasting, buddy?"

"Wendy, I need some advice," Mabel said. "You've broken up with guys, right?"

"Oh, yeah." She started to count on her fingers. "Russ Durham, Eli Hall, Stony Davidson—"

"I don't know what's wrong with me!" Mabel wailed. "I thought everything was back to normal, but I still feel all gross."

"—Mike Worley, Nate Holts. Oh, that guy with the tattoos," Wendy said, still counting.

Mabel sighed. "Maybe letting Dipper do it for me was a mistake. Gideon deserves an honest breakup."

"Danny Feldman, Mark Epstein—oh man, I'm not sure I ever actually broke up with him. No wonder he keeps calling me!"

"I know what I gotta do," Mabel said. "Thanks for talking to me, Wendy!"

She hopped on her bike and pedaled away.

Wendy's phone beeped. It was one of her exes. "Ignore!"

Over at the factory, Dipper was dodging Lil' Gideon merchandise as the tiny psychic hurled the floating objects at him one by one. They shattered down around him. He ran toward a huge bookcase, which came crashing down toward him. Dipper rolled away just in time.

"Grunkle Stan was right about you!" Dipper yelled. "You are a monster!"

"Your sister will be mine!" cried Gideon, laughing maniacally.

Gideon pulled a string on his doll and it mimicked his laugh.

Glancing down, Dipper saw a box labeled LIL'
GIDEON BRAND BLUNT OBJECT. He reached inside
and pulled out a baseball bat, charging Gideon.
Gideon pointed a finger and sent Dipper floating
in the air.

"She's never gonna date you, man!" Dipper
yelled.

"That's a lie!" Gideon roared. "And I'm gonna
make sure you never lie to me again, friend."

He nodded toward a box of LIL' GIDEON LAMB
SHEARS. The box opened by itself and a pair of
sharp shears floated up and started snapping
menacingly at Dipper.

Mabel burst through the door of the warehouse. "Gideon! We have to talk!"

Gideon spun around, surprised. "M-M-Mabel! My marshmallow! What are you doing here?" he stuttered, and the shears clattered harmlessly to the floor.

"I'm sorry, Gideon, but I can't be your marshmallow," Mabel said. "I needed to be honest and tell you that myself."

"I don't understand," he said, anxiously grasping the stone in his bolo tie. The blue-green energy cloud around Dipper started to sizzle.

"Uh, Mabel, this probably isn't the best time to be brutally honest with him!" Dipper called down as he felt an invisible force choke him.

Mabel took a step toward Gideon, smiling sweetly. "Hey, but we can still be makeover buddies, right?" she asked Gideon. "Wouldn't you like that?"

Gideon's eyes widened. "Really?" he asked.

"No! Not really!" Mabel cried, yanking the bolo tie off his neck.

The blue-green light vanished and Dipper fell to the floor.

"You were, like, attacking my brother!" said Mabel. "What the heck!"

"My tie! Give it back!" Gideon demanded.

He lunged for Mabel, who tossed the stone to Dipper.

"Hah! Not so powerful without this, are you?" Dipper asked.

Gideon charged at Dipper like a bull. Dipper tossed the stone back to Mabel just as Gideon rammed into him. He and Gideon crashed through the factory window off an enormous cliff!

"Dipper!" Mabel yelled.

As they plummeted off the cliff, Gideon and Dipper traded slaps. Then they noticed the ground coming up to meet them. They were doomed!

"Aaaaaaaaaah!" they screamed.

Then a blue-green light surrounded them, suspending them in midair. They looked up to see Mabel floating in the air above them, bathed in light. The stone glowed in her hand.

"Listen, Gideon. It's over. I will never, ever date you," Mabel said.

"Yeah!" shouted Dipper as he and Gideon fell to the ground.

Then Mabel threw the stone against a rock and it crumbled into dust.

"My powers!" Gideon wailed. His eyes narrowed as he backed away. "Oh, this isn't over. This isn't the last you'll see of widdle ol' me."

Gideon angrily marched back home and

pushed open the door, where he found his father and Stan relaxing on the couch, drinking name-brand soda and planning a profitable future together.

Gideon jumped up on the coffee table and pointed at Stan. "Stanford Pines, I rebuke thee! I rebuke thee!"

"'Rebuke'? Is that a word?" Stan asked.

"The entire Pines family has invoked my fury! You will all pay recompense for your transgressions!" Gideon said, clenching his fists.

"What, you got like a word-a-day calendar or something?" Stan asked.

Buddy nervously wrung his hands together and addressed Gideon. "But, sunshine, what about our arrangement with Mabel and the—"

"Silence!" Gideon roared at him.

Buddy chuckled and turned to Stan. "Well, uh, I see he's taken to one of his *rages* again. Sorry, Stan. I have to side with Gideon on this one."

He tore up the contract that he and Stan had drafted.

Stan stood up. "Okay! Okay! I can see when I'm not wanted."

Then Stan grabbed the sad clown painting from the wall and hot-footed it out the door.

"Try and catch me, suckers!" he yelled out behind him.

Stan jumped in his car and raced back to the Mystery Shack, where he found Dipper and Mabel sitting forlornly on the couch.

"I could have had it all," Stan said with a sigh as he mounted the sad clown painting on the wall. Then he noticed how miserable Dipper and Mabel both looked.

"What the heck happened to you two?"

"Gideon," the twins said together.

Stan squinted his eyes. "Gideon. Yeah. The little mutant swore vengeance on the whole family." Stan chuckled. "I guess he's gonna try to nibble my ankles or something."

Dipper brightened. Grunkle Stan had a point. Without his magic stone, Gideon was just an annoying kid. "Oh, yeah. How's he gonna destroy us now? Try to guess what number we're thinking of?" Dipper laughed.

"He'll never guess what number I'm thinking of," Mabel said. "Negative eight! No one would guess a negative number!"

They all laughed.

"Look out! Bet he's planning our destruction right now!" Stan said, and they all laughed even harder.

But in fact, Gideon *was* planning their destruction. . . .

"Gideon, I still love you!" Gideon said in a high voice, holding up a Mabel figurine he had made out of wood. "If only my family wasn't in the way."

Then he picked up a figurine that looked like Stan. "Look at me, I am old! And I'm smelly!"

Finally, he picked up a Dipper figurine. "Hey, what are you gonna do without your precious amulet?"

Gideon grinned. "Oh, you'll see, boy. You'll see. . . ."